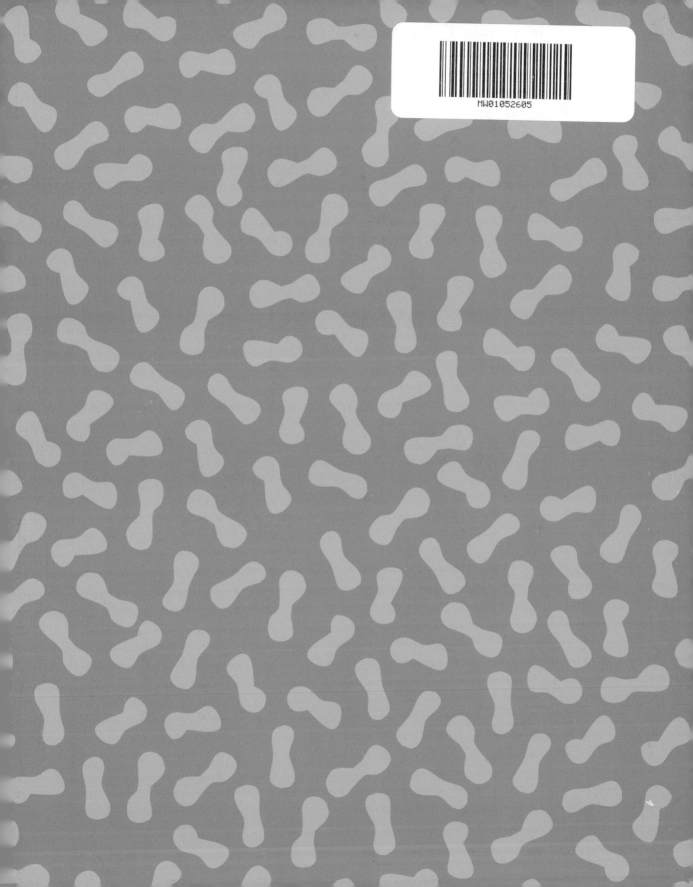

To our son Davis,
thank you for making our lives a
constant adventure.

Books may be purchased in quantity and/or special sales by contacting the publisher, Louie's Little Lessons, at hello@louieslittlelessons.com.

Published in San Diego, California by Louie's Little Lessons. Louie's Little Lessons is a registered trademark.

Illustrations by: Greg Bishop
Interior Design by: Ron Eddy
Cover Design by: Greg Bishop and Ron Eddy
Editing by: Julie Breihan

Printed in China

ISBN: 978-0-9981936-2-5

Louie's Little Lessons

I'M THE POTTY MASTER!

written by **Liz Fletcher**   illustrated by **Greg Bishop**

High up in his treehouse,
Louie swings beneath the leaves.

He feels free
and happy,
His cape sailing in
the breeze.

Louie is getting bigger.
He's a superhero too,

Saving friends from
furry monsters.

"Watch out, I'm
coming through!"

"Wait a second! Time out!"
Louie's diaper is in the way.

He needs
to have it
changed
If he wants to
save the day!

Maybe without diapers
Louie could play for hours on end.
Without stopping to be changed
He'd have more time with friends!

Perhaps Louie would feel lighter,
Swinging high above the ground.

He could launch up to the airplanes

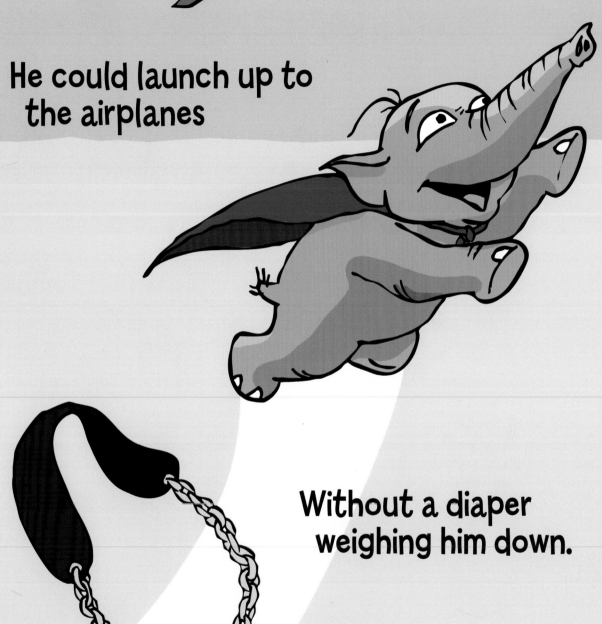

Without a diaper weighing him down.

Louie could blast off like a rocket
And save the day a lot faster.

Without a dirty diaper
He'd be the potty master!

Hmmm, Louie thinks,
I just don't know what to do.

Maybe I should stop
wearing diapers,

But I'm unsure
about trying
something new.

Big kids use the potty.
Mommy and Daddy do too.
It seems pretty easy.
"What do YOU think I
    should do?"

Louie fastens his cape tightly.
He can feel his superpowers grow.

"Okay, I think I'll try it
Because I really have to go!"

He pulls down his diaper,
Then he sits and waits . . .
Louie hears a tinkle and a toot.
"I did it! Wow, this feels great!"

"I'm a big kid now!
New undies, here I come!
(I picked the ones with peanuts.)
Now there's more time for fun!"

Sometimes
accidents happen,
But Louie keeps on trying

Because every day he gets better,
And then there's more time for flying!

Change is so very important.
Louie is glad he tried something new.
He loves using the potty,
And you know what, you will too!

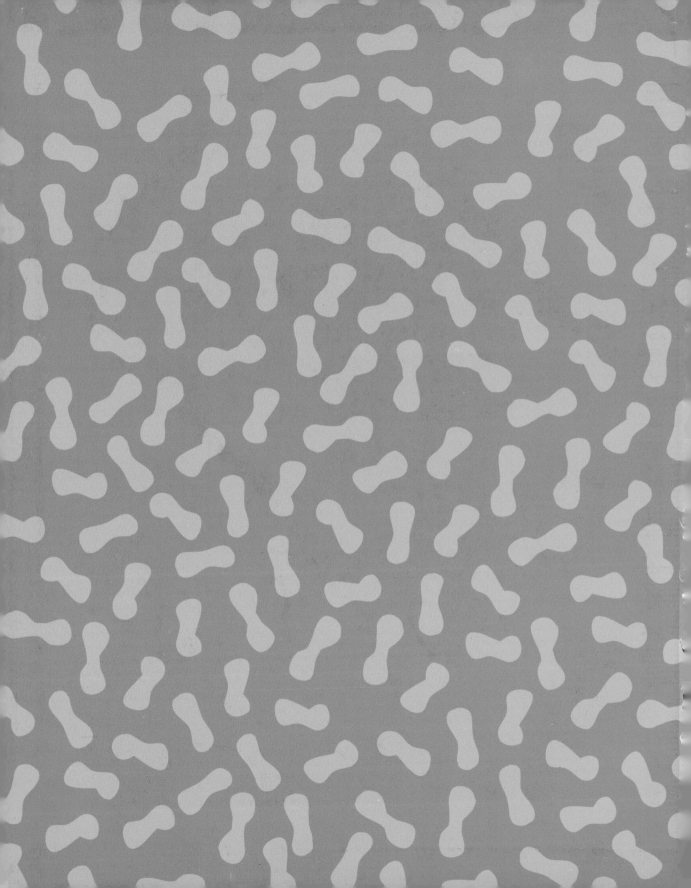